The
MAFIA
Incident

Other books in this series:
THE WOLLAGONG INCIDENT
THE BERMUDA TRIANGLE INCIDENT
THE CIRCLE OF DEATH INCIDENT
THE BORLEY RECTORY INCIDENT
THE TRANSYLVANIAN INCIDENT
THE EASTER ISLAND INCIDENT
THE PYRAMID INCIDENT
THE CHINESE GHOST INCIDENT

TERRANCE DICKS

The
MAFIA
Incident

Piccadilly Press • London

Phototypeset from author's disk by Piccadilly Press.
Printed and bound by Creative Print and Design (Wales),
Ebbw Vale, for the publishers Piccadilly Press Ltd.,
5 Castle Road, London NW1 8PR

A catalogue record for this book is available from
the British Library

ISBNs: 1 85340 665 1 (trade paperback)

3 5 7 9 10 8 6 4 2

Terrance Dicks lives in North London. He has written many books
for Piccadilly Press including the CHANGING UNIVERSE series, the
HARVEY series, THE GOOD, THE BAD AND THE GHASTLY series and
the SECOND SIGHT series.

Cover design by Judith Robertson

PROLOGUE

The temple stood in a shallow basin some distance from the nearest town.

Although it was over a thousand years old, it looked whole. Its thirty-six regularly-spaced stone columns were all intact, the surrounding pediments undamaged.

Although the temple had no roof, it was not so much ruined as unfinished. Some long-ago local war had broken out soon after work on the temple had begun. The building had never been completed.

In the daytime tourists roamed freely through the sun-bleached interior, sending lizards scampering over the yellow pitted stone, disturbing the birds that nested on the high columns.

Now, in the moonlight, the temple was peaceful and undisturbed. At night it was once more a place of power. Few cared to disturb its brooding silence – especially on the night of the full moon.

But one man came.

Young and handsome, dressed in shabby, well-worn clothes, he moved easily along the path that led down to the temple. When he reached the temple he strode inside, his booted feet ringing confidently on the flagstones.

He paused near the centre of the temple, looking around him. He began chanting in a deep, compelling voice.

The incantation came to an end, and he waited expectantly. For a moment nothing happened.

Then, from out of nowhere, a wind swept through the temple. A glowing circle of light appeared on the time-worn flagstones.

The young man chanted again, strange, sonorous words in some ancient tongue.

The figure of an old woman appeared from the shadows. She was very tall and very thin in long black robes. Grey hair streamed behind her in the sudden wind.

Behind her stood a thin dark girl robed in flowing white.

The old woman spoke, her voice a harsh, grating croak. 'Who summons me?'

'I summon you,' said the young man. For all

his apparent confidence, his voice trembled a little.

'What do you seek?'

'I seek the Power.'

'Fool!' said the old woman. 'The Power will only destroy you.'

'I will take that risk.'

'Will you lose your soul?'

'My soul is my own to risk.'

There was a long pause. The old woman said, 'You speak the Words of Power. I may not deny you. Come forward at your own risk!'

He walked forward into the glowing circle. A pillar of light sprang up around him.

The old woman walked into it, stretched out a skinny hand and touched his forehead. Her touch felt icy cold – yet it burned at the same time. Fire flowed through his body, as if the blood in his veins glowed red-hot. The pain was indescribable, but the young man stood motionless.

'You have courage at least,' said the old woman reluctantly. She removed her hand and the fire died away.

The young man shuddered, his face streaming with sweat. 'Is it done?' he asked hoarsely.

'The Power is yours – for a time. But it must

be renewed. You must come here again at the next full moon, and for one more full moon after that.'

'And after the third moon the Power will be mine to hold?'

'The Power will be yours to keep – or it will destroy you. Few can bear the full burden of the Goddess's Power.'

'Very well,' said the young man calmly. 'I return at the next full moon.'

The glowing circle disappeared. The black-robed figure and the white-clad girl faded back into the shadows.

The young man heard a sound behind him and whirled round. A snake was slithering across the stone floor. He shot out his hand, pointing a finger, and the snake exploded in flame.

The young man looked at the blackened remains of the snake for a moment. They lay on the scorched flagstones like a piece of charred and twisted rope.

With an exultant laugh he turned and strode away.

Chapter One

CONFERENCE IN SICILY

'Thirty years!' said Dad scornfully. 'Thirty years since man set foot on the moon for the first time. Twenty-seven years since the last moon landing in 1972!' His angry gaze swept scornfully round the crowded lecture room. 'A pitiful total of six manned landings in all. Since then – nothing. Nothing – for over a quarter of a century!'

His audience hung its collective head guiltily.

'As so often happens,' Dad went on, 'mankind had done the right thing for all the wrong reasons. Alarmed by the success of Russian space probes, the Americans decided they had to catch up – not only catch up, but decisively overtake! Inspired by interplanetary road rage, President Kennedy poured resources into putting a man on the moon before the Russians. Once success was achieved, superiority demonstrated, enthusiasm waned.

With the end of the Cold War, the old rivalry wasn't there any more. Oh, space research of a sort continued. Satellites, unmanned probes, Mir Space Station orbiting the earth like a bucket of rusty bolts. But think what should have happened! By now there should be a long-established moon base. By now we should be launching a manned rocket to Mars. Not in pursuit of petty nationalist rivalry – but because escape from this overcrowded, polluted planet is the only hope for the future of mankind!'

The audience clapped and cheered. Mind you, it was a pretty good lecture. The trouble was, I'd heard it many times before, very often directed at me alone.

I took advantage of the excitement to get up – I'd been careful to choose an aisle seat right at the back – and sidled towards the door.

Dad reduced his audience to silence with an upraised hand. 'And how is all this to be achieved? I will tell you!'

And he will too, I thought, as I slipped through the lecture-room door. And at some length as well.

Fond as I was of the old boy, I couldn't face hearing it all again. Walking quickly and decisively, like a man with a mission, I crossed the marbled foyer of the lecture hall and went out into the blazing sunshine of Palermo.

Nobody tried to stop me.

I'm Matt Stirling.

The tall, bespectacled, beaky-nosed character holding forth inside the lecture hall was my father, Professor James Stirling, world-famous space scientist and all-round egghead.

Due to the drying-up of funds for space research, he'd been sidetracked into taking a job as Director of Paranormal Studies for an American research institute.

At the same time, he'd been landed with responsibility for a teenage son – me – whom he hadn't seen since babyhood.

He'd coped by taking me out of school and making me his assistant. He himself was looking after my education, grooming me for university.

Dad was a one-man college all by himself.

As a result of all this, my life had changed dramatically. The paranormal research job had taken us into some strange places, and I'd undergone some weird experiences.

Weirdest of all had been living and working with a father I hardly knew. It wasn't always an easy relationship, but we'd come to a kind of understanding.

Dad is noisy, bad-tempered, arrogant and obstinate, expecting to get his own way as a matter of course.

I'm quieter on the surface, but pretty strong-willed underneath. At least, I call it strong-willed. Dad has other terms – like 'pigheaded', 'incredibly insolent' or 'stubborn as a mule'.

It all depends on your point of view.

I crossed the paved courtyard, went through ornate iron gates, and found myself in the baking-hot streets of Palermo, capital of Sicily.

I still couldn't believe I was really there.

It had all started a few weeks before, over breakfast in our top-floor flat overlooking Hampstead Heath.

Dad was opening his mail, filing it in his usual efficient manner. He ripped open each envelope, skimmed through the contents, snarled, screwed up letter and envelope, then hurled them towards the wastepaper basket, missing every time.

He shoved his cup towards me and grunted, 'Coffee.'

I shoved it back at him and grunted, 'Percolator.'

You had to take a firm line with Dad. He was used to teams of dedicated research assistants dancing round him, eager to fulfil his every whim.

Now there was only me – and I wasn't up for the job of Jeeves.

Dad looked up and gave me his famous withering glare. It had reduced generations of lab assistants to jelly – but I'd been glared at so much by now I was fireproof.

I grinned cheerfully back at him.

Dad sighed. 'I beg your pardon, Matthew. Could I possibly trouble you to pour me another cup of coffee while I deal with the rest of my important correspondence?'

'With pleasure, Father.' I poured him another cup of coffee. I'm slowly getting him civilised.

Dad was opening the last envelope, an elaborate-looking affair in expensive-looking parchment.

He took out a sheet of equally expensive-looking writing paper with some kind of embossed heading and studied it.

This time he didn't screw it up. He read it through again and then put the letter reverently on the table.

'What is it?' I asked.

'It's from the University of Palermo.'

'What about?'

'Apparently they're opening a new science wing. They're holding an opening conference.'

'So?'

'They've invited me to be their guest of honour – to deliver a short series of inaugural lectures. They want to present me with an honorary degree.'

There was something strange about the way Dad looked and it took me a moment to realise what it was. The old devil was actually blushing!

Of course there was still quite a bit of huffing and puffing after that. Dad started saying how busy he was, and how he didn't know if he could fit it in.

Pure nonsense, of course. Things had been rather quiet since our trip to Egypt. Besides, it was only first-night nerves. He wouldn't have missed it for the world.

I wasn't a bit surprised when he finally

accepted the invitation. What did surprise me was his asking me to go with him.

'That is if you'd care to, Matthew,' he said offhandedly. 'I shall be tied up a lot of the time, of course. But Sicily is a fascinating island, and you're old enough to do a bit of sightseeing on your own. And I'd be free most evenings.'

He went on shuffling the lecture notes he was preparing, as if he couldn't care less whether I came with him or not.

'Thanks,' I said. 'I'd like to come very much.'

He looked up and nodded and went on with his work. I think he was pleased; it's hard to tell with Dad. You can always tell when he's not pleased though . . .

A few weeks after that, we caught the plane to Palermo.

Two and a half hours later we landed at Falcone Berlusconi Airport in Punta Raisi, which is thirty kilometres west of the city.

'It's named after a couple of magistrates who got bumped off by the Mafia,' I told Dad as we got off the plane. As usual, I'd done some research on our destination.

Dad sniffed. 'Too many late-night films, Matthew,' he said. 'All this Mafia nonsense is vastly exaggerated, you know.'

I didn't bother to argue with him. If he liked to think the Mafia was a Hollywood myth, so much the better, it was probably safer that way. Besides, he was right in a way; there was no reason for us to be concerned. As my guide book said, the Mafia has little relevance for casual travellers.

If only I'd known . . .

We found a delegation waiting at the airport to welcome the distinguished *professore* and his completely undistinguished son. We were whisked away in a limousine to one of Palermo's best hotels, then on to the university for a reception.

Two members of the science faculty had been delegated to look after us.

The elder, Professore Arturo Baldovino, was small and tubby, with big round spectacles and a bushy beard.

His assistant, Dottore Fabio Casale, was slim and elegant, a small but perfectly formed Latin lover type in an Armani suit.

Since their names and titles were such a

mouthful, I decided to think of them as Arturo and Fabio.

Both were elaborately polite, and couldn't do enough for us.

Next morning they collected us at the hotel and whisked us off to the university for Dad's opening speech. It was a fairly brief affair. He said how honoured he was by the invitation, and sketched out the ground he was going to cover.

After a lavish buffet lunch came the real lecture – the one I'd just ducked out of. I reckoned I'd done my duty by attending the first two affairs. As I said, I'd heard it all before. Besides which, there was no one remotely near my own age around and nobody was really interested in me anyway.

To make matters worse, Dad had made me swap my usual jeans and T-shirt for a blazer and trousers, complete with collar and tie.

'Things are more formal on the Continent, Matthew,' he said.

He'd tried to get me to wear a suit, but I wasn't having that. Blazer and trousers is as formal as I get.

I yanked off the tie and stuck it in my pocket as

I walked away from the university. My plan was just to explore the neighbourhood a bit and try my phrase-book Italian in some café. I reckoned Dad's lecture was good for at least an hour, and I planned to be back by the time he finished.

I'd expected the university to be in one of the posher parts of town, and I was surprised by the scruffiness of the surrounding streets. Some of the buildings were boarded up and there were still actual bomb-sites to be seen, left over from World War Two.

I knew the reason for that.

After the war lots of foreign-aid money flooded into Europe to rebuild the shattered cities. Here a lot of that money melted mysteriously away, allegedly into the pockets of the Mafia. As a result, Palermo is one of the few European cities still showing some of the scars of war – fifty odd years afterwards.

I seemed to have got myself into an area of warehouses with not a shop or a café in sight. Then I spotted a busier looking area at the end of a long narrow sidestreet, and made my way towards it.

A high wall with a gate in it lined the left-hand

side of the street. As I walked towards the gate it opened, and a man came out. He looked impatiently up and down the street, and then looked at his watch. Clearly someone was late.

The man had something slung over his shoulder. At first I thought it was a shoulder bag. Then I realised it was a shotgun.

Some kind of security guard, no doubt, I thought idly. But then where was his uniform?

Perhaps security guards didn't wear uniforms in Sicily. Or perhaps he wasn't a security guard.

Hadn't I read somewhere that the shotgun, the *lupara*, was the traditional weapon of the Mafia foot-soldier?

At this point a battered grey Fiat van roared round the corner, zoomed past me and pulled up at the gate. The waiting guard shouted angrily at the driver. The driver yelled back.

The guard gestured impatiently at the open gate. Clearly the van was supposed to drive through.

This was going to be easier said than done. Even from a distance I could see that the gateway wasn't very much wider than the van. Judging by his angry gestures, the van driver thought so as well.

There was a further angry exchange and then the driver reversed his van into the road, presumably to get a clear run at the gate. He began driving slowly towards it – assisted by the guard with encouraging gestures and shouted instructions – presumably the Italian equivalent of 'Left hand down a bit!'

It didn't work out. The van hit the left-hand gatepost. The guard yelled a protest, pointing out what the van had done to his gate. The driver jumped out and pointed out, with impassioned anger, what the gatepost had done to his van.

They went on yelling at each other for a bit. Then the driver got back into his van, backed off and had another try. The van drove very slowly through the gate with only centimetres to spare and disappeared inside.

I'd stopped walking to watch this bit of Sicilian street theatre. Now I walked on, thinking how much you could understand without speaking the language. The gate was still open as I came level with it, and I glanced curiously inside.

I should have remembered what curiosity did to the cat.

The gate gave on to a cobbled yard, with a tall

warehouse building on the other side. The van was parked in front of the warehouse door and the rear doors were open.

The driver was in the back of the van, passing a long, canvas-wrapped bundle down to the guard. They seemed to be having quite a struggle. It was clear that the bundle was very heavy.

The guard still had his shotgun slung over his shoulder and it made him clumsy. Somehow his arm got tangled in the sling and he lost his grip on his end of the bundle. It fell to the cobbles and the canvas unrolled, revealing what was inside.

It was a bulky, metallic, tubular affair, painted dark green. It had a carrying-handle, a shoulder-stock and some kind of sighting device on the broad metal barrel.

It was the sort of thing you see soldiers lugging about in documentaries on civil war in Africa.

It was some kind of one-man anti-tank weapon. A rocket-launcher.

I stood, staring at it in astonishment – and the two men by the van looked up and saw me.

The guard started to untangle his shotgun. I ran for my life.

Chapter Two

HUNTED

I ran on down the narrow street and into the wider one that cut across it at right angles. It seemed to be some kind of local high street. There was a little market in the middle, crowded with Sicilian mums buying their fruit and veg. Most of them wore black, and I remembered reading that in some Sicilian villages *all* the women wore black, because everyone had lost someone in a local blood feud.

I noticed a strange little stall. It was selling a variety of trinkets and amulets. Many of them carried the weird circular symbol which I knew to be a charm against the evil eye – still greatly feared in Sicily. For some reason, a little chill ran down my spine.

I turned left, more or less at random, and hurried as fast as I could through the market, muttering *'Scusi, scusi,'* as I pushed my way through the shoppers.

There was a striped awning on the next corner and a scattering of rusty iron chairs and tables. Still acting on impulse, I hurried towards the café and went inside.

Inside it was dark and gloomy and it took a moment for my eyes to adjust from the bright sunshine outside. There wasn't much to see: a bar across the back wall with a huge espresso machine behind it, and an even more huge barman in a grimy apron. There were wooden chairs and tables occupied by tough-looking, swarthy, un-shaven characters, like extras from *The Godfather*.

I told myself not to give way to racial stereo-typing. No doubt they were all perfectly respectable family men.

Everyone stared at me unblinkingly. In my natty blazer and trousers I looked and felt utterly out of place, like an English twit in some old comedy movie.

I went up to the bar. '*Espresso doppio, per favore.*'

The barman stared at me, as if amazed that I could actually speak. Barrel-shaped, balding and bristly-chinned, he looked tougher than his cus-tomers – which was saying something.

He grunted and turned to his machine. After a

vast amount of hissing and clanking he slapped a thick white cup down in front of me. A large black coffee. Exactly what I needed to steady my nerves.

I sipped my coffee and thought about my next move. It was obvious. Get the hell out of there, back to the university.

But how? Out on the street I ran the risk of running into the man with the shotgun and his mate. I had a pretty good idea that they'd be out looking for me by now.

I felt in my blazer pocket and took out my Italian minidictionary. I found the useful phrases section and studied it, expecting to find 'My aunt has the pen of the gardener' and 'Stop the coach, the postillion has been struck by lightning'.

Instead I found exactly what I needed. I turned back to the barman. '*Può chiamarmi un taxi, per favore?*'

The barman looked outraged. It was pretty clear that taxi-calling for customers wasn't a normal part of his duties.

I reached into my back pocket and pulled out my little bundle of Italian lire. I fished out a note at random and pushed it towards him. He stared at it in amazement.

Deciding to play it safe, I selected an even bigger note and put it on top of the first. '*Un taxi*,' I repeated firmly. '*Pronto, per favore!*'

It did the trick. Clearly deciding I was an eccentric English millionaire, the barman said, '*Si, signore, un taxi, subito!*' He produced a telephone from under the bar, dialled, and muttered into it.

'*Grazie, signore*,' I said graciously. I took my cup to a table near the door and settled down to wait. I sipped the thick black coffee and looked up and down the colourful little street.

In a way it was hard to believe I was in any real danger. It was such an everyday scene. Mums shopping, kids playing, youths chatting on street corners, dogs dozing in the sunshine.

But I'm the careful type and, as I said, I'd made it a point to do some research on Sicily and the Mafia. I knew its influence ranged right through Sicilian society, from the very rich to the poorest of the poor. Its power reached out from Sicily to Italy and to the government in Rome.

An organisation that had blown up or shot down dozens of examining magistrates and senior policemen wasn't going to be too bothered about disposing of one obscure English tourist.

I was pretty sure that the Mafia must be involved in what I'd seen. Who else would want a rocket-launcher? And, come to that, what did they want it for?

I hadn't yet decided what, if anything, I was going to do about what I'd seen. My first priority was getting back to Dad and the university alive. Or I wouldn't be able to do anything . . .

Glancing to my left I saw the welcome sign of a taxi turning into the street.

Looking to the right, I saw something a lot less welcome. The two men from the warehouse were moving along the street towards me. The gate guard wasn't carrying his shotgun – but that didn't mean there wasn't something equally dangerous under his ragged coat. The two were looking all around them. It was pretty clear that they were hunting for someone.

Me.

I was tempted to jump up and run for the approaching taxi, but decided against it. Wild animals freeze when they feel under threat. As it says in all those David Attenborough wildlife documentaries, it's the sudden movement of the prey that attracts the hunter.

I slouched down in my chair, hoping the darkness of the bar made me invisible from the sunny street outside. It's hard to see from bright light into semi-darkness.

From where I sat I could see the taxi slowly making its way along the crowded street, with much honking of its horn. From the other direction, the two Mafiosi shouldered their way through the crowd, peering suspiciously around them.

I was tempted to lie low and hope they went by – but if they stopped to check the café I'd be trapped. Besides, they'd be sure to notice when the taxi pulled up at the café.

I waited till the taxi drew level with the café and stopped. Then I jumped out of my chair, ran out of the café and sprinted towards it.

Snatching open the rear passenger door I jumped inside. *'Università di Palermo!'* I yelled. *'Pronto, per favore!'*

To my horror the taxi didn't move. The driver looked over his shoulder and gave out a stream of angry Italian. *'Riservato!'* he yelled. *'Riservato!'*

Suddenly I realised – he was telling me the taxi was already booked. Abandoning the Italian language I yelled, 'Look, *I* booked this taxi. The barman phoned from the café for me!'

Fortunately, the driver spoke English. '*You* book taxi?'

'That's right. Palermo University, please – and hurry.'

'Hokey-dokey!'

We set off again, moving as fast as was possible along the crowded street. I heard a sudden shout and looked out of the window. The two Mafiosi were running after the cab. As I'd feared, they'd spotted me when I left the café.

Since the taxi was only crawling, they caught up with it easily enough. I tried to lock the door, but I was just too late. The one in the lead, the gate guard, flung open the door and tried to drag me out.

I pressed myself back in the corner, raised both feet, planted them in his stomach and heaved. I'm big and strong for my age and he was only a skinny little chap. He flew backwards through the air and crashed into the second Mafioso close behind him. They both fell into a fruit stall, bringing the whole thing to the ground.

Fruit and veg and angry customers were

strewn everywhere, and an instant riot sprang up.

'Hey, what's going on?' yelled the taxi driver.

'You don't want to know,' I told him, desperately shoving a handful of lire at him. 'And you don't want to get mixed up in it either. Just get me out of here. Take me to the university, then forget all about it!'

'Hokey-dokey,' said the driver again.

Since the road was filled with a struggling, shouting crowd, he screeched up on to a bit of empty pavement, swung back on the road again and hurtled around the corner.

Twenty minutes later he was dropping me at the university gates. The taxi roared away and I went inside the building.

I slipped back into the lecture hall, just in time to hear Dad saying, 'Those, then, are the problems of a revitalised space programme. As you can see, there are many, both technological and financial. Tomorrow, I hope to offer you some solutions. If the will is there, all problems can be overcome.'

There was a round of applause, slightly more subdued this time. The lecture room was hot, and the audience was tiring a bit. Dad left the platform and was immediately surrounded by a congratulatory group of officials, the tubby Professore Arturo Baldovino and the elegant Dottore Fabio Casale prominent amongst them.

I heard cries of *'Bravo, professore, bravissimo!'* and *'Eccezionale!'*

I waited until the audience had finished shuffling out, and went over to join the little group. I couldn't compete with Italian enthusiasm so I delivered my congratulations with typically British reserve. 'Well done, Dad. A great success.'

'Especially the beginning and the end?' said Dad drily. He doesn't miss much.

There was a lot more congratulatory chatter, and then the car arrived to take us back to the hotel.

Once we were settled in the back of the limousine, gliding through the shabby streets, Dad said, 'And now, Matthew, perhaps you'll tell me what happened between your leaving the lecture hall and your timely return?'

The sudden question caught me by surprise. 'What makes you think anything happened?' I said feebly.

'You came back into the hall like a rabbit

bolting back down its hole. You were tense, looking all around you all the way out to the car. I can *feel* the strain in you now.'

I take back what I said about him not missing much. He doesn't miss *anything*.

I'd thought I was playing it pretty cool myself. Then again, maybe being chased by a couple of Mafia thugs had shaken me up more than I'd thought.

I tried playing for time. 'All right, so I went for a wander round. I got into a pretty tough area, felt a bit threatened and made my way back. Nothing actually *happened* . . .'

It's never easy putting anything over Dad. In fact, it's practically impossible. We know each other too well now. He looked hard at me for a moment, and then shook his head. 'There was more to it than that. Please don't lie to me, Matthew, it's not like you.'

'It's not a matter of lying,' I said. 'I just don't want to talk about it right now.' I glanced uneasily at the partition that separated us from the uniformed chauffeur. 'Look, let's just leave it for now. I'll tell you later, back at the hotel.'

'Very well.' Dad gave an offended nod and

began checking the papers in his briefcase. We passed the rest of the journey in silence.

Back at the hotel we were whisked up to our luxurious suite. I showered and put on a clean shirt. I had to stick with the hated blazer and trousers. Professore Arturo Baldovino and Dottore Fabio Casale were taking us out to dinner that night, and I had strict instructions to stay dressed up.

When I emerged into our shared sitting-room, Dad was investigating the contents of the minibar. He straightened up with a bottle of Coke in one hand and a half-bottle of red wine in the other.

He passed me the Coke and poured himself a glass of wine. 'Now, Matthew,' he said firmly.

I could tell by the look in his eye that there was no point in arguing. I told him the whole story.

He listened intently, without interruptions. And he didn't insult my intelligence by suggesting I was either imagining or exaggerating things.

When I'd finished he sat silently for a moment. Then he said, 'You're sure about the weapon?'

'I'm sure about the kind of weapon,' I said. 'I've seen the things on telly dozens of times. Every tin-pot rebel guerilla seems to have one. I can't tell you the model or the make or anything. It had a sort of war-surplus look, that's all.'

'You should have told me this at once, back at the university,' said Dad severely. 'We must go to the police.'

'I knew you'd say that,' I said. 'That's just why I didn't tell you.'

'I don't understand.'

I sighed. 'Firstly, there's a good chance they won't believe me. I *know* I saw two Mafia thugs with a rocket-launcher. Suppose they decide I saw two workmen unloading a drainpipe?'

'Then that's their responsibility,' said Dad promptly. 'It's still our responsibility to give them the information.'

'There's something else,' I said.

'Like what?'

'Suppose they do believe I've stumbled on to some kind of Mafia plot. Now you know about it too. Do you know what happens to people who know too much about the Mafia in Palermo?'

'So that's why you didn't want to tell me,' said Dad slowly. 'You were trying to keep me out of danger . . .'

'I'm trying to keep us both out of danger,' I said

frankly. 'I'm not sure we shouldn't just catch the first plane home! I'll write a letter to the police when we're safely back.'

'Impossible,' said Dad firmly. 'The information might arrive too late to be of any use. Besides, I have obligations to the university. And we both have obligations to law and order, to common justice.' Dad shook his head. 'We must go to the police at once.'

'Even at the risk of getting ourselves killed?'

'Yes,' said Dad firmly. 'Even at the risk of getting ourselves killed.'

Chapter Three

THE PLOT

You had to admire the old boy, I thought. He was brave, he had noble principles – and in some things he was totally dumb. Not in the sense of being stupid, nobody could call him that. More like blinkered. He was brilliant in his own field – but there were areas of life he knew little or nothing about.

Part of the problem was that he thought everywhere was like dear old England. If you saw someone breaking the law you went straight to the police. Then they sent Dixon of Dock Green around on a bike to sort things out. Even England wasn't like that any more – if it ever had been. And in other parts of the world, things could be very different indeed.

The trouble with Dad was he didn't really *believe* in the Mafia. To him it only existed in late-night crime movies – the kind he disapproved of me watching.

I knew better. The power of the Mafia stretched all over Italy, and over much of America as well. Here in Sicily, in Palermo, we were in its birthplace, the place where it was strongest.

'All right,' I said. 'We'll go to the authorities. But I don't fancy wandering into the nearest police station with a tale like this. Especially as neither of us speaks much Italian. We'd be there all night before we found someone to listen to us.' I sighed. 'Sitting on hard wooden chairs in some sordid interview room while they sent out for an interpreter. Writing out endless statements . . .'

Dad scowled. He may have high principles, but he also has a high regard for his own comfort. He'd been looking forward to a nice dinner and a night's sleep in a comfortable bed. My alternative scenario didn't have much appeal.

'There's something in what you say,' he admitted. 'What do you suggest?'

'The Super Mario brothers will be here before long.'

Dad looked outraged. '*Who* will be here?' He doesn't approve of computer games either.

'Bill and Ben,' I said. 'Mutt and Jeff. The Chuckle brothers. You know, our two Italian minders.

They're taking us out to dinner, remember?'

'I take it you are referring to Professore Arturo Baldovino and Dottore Fabio Casale?' he said frostily.

'That's right.'

'Well? What about them?'

'They're supposed to be looking after us, aren't they? Let's ask their advice.'

Dad frowned. 'They're scientists, academics. How can they help with something like this?'

'They're still part of the establishment here in Palermo,' I pointed out. 'They're bound to know someone in authority. At the very least they'll know someone who knows someone. Someone senior who can make sure we're taken seriously.'

Dad still looked dubious, so I added the clincher. 'After all, you're an honoured guest of the university. A VIP. You shouldn't have to deal with the common *carabinieri*. You need to talk to the Chief of Police.'

That did the trick. 'Very well, we'll do as you suggest. But I'll thank you not to make up disrespectful nicknames for my academic colleagues. Super Mario brothers, indeed!' Dad took a swig of his wine. 'Laurel and Hardy possibly . . .'

We finished our drinks and went down to the hotel lobby to meet the dynamic duo.

They arrived in a state of great excitement.

'Wonderful news, *professore*, wonderful news,' said tubby little Arturo. 'Senator Salvatore Lupo has agreed to attend the closing ceremony, after your final lecture. He himself will present you with your honorary degree on behalf of the university.'

He looked at us hopefully, clearly expecting us to share his delight.

'Forgive me,' said Dad. 'I'm afraid my knowledge of Italian politics is sadly deficient. Senator Lupo, you said?'

'He is the newly appointed head of the Palermo Anti-Mafia Commission,' said the elegant Fabio reproachfully. 'It was my idea to invite him. Nobody thought he would come.'

'His acceptance of our invitation is a very great honour,' said Arturo. 'He attends very few public events. He lives a somewhat secluded life.'

I bet he does! I thought. Surrounded by stone walls, barbed-wire and bodyguards.

Being in the Anti-Mafia Commission wasn't the

healthiest job in the world. Many of its members had been shot down or blown up over the years. Like Falcone and Berlusconi, the two magistrates they'd named the airport after.

Mention of the commission reminded both me and Dad of the problem on our minds. Maybe this was the answer. We exchanged glances, both wondering whether to speak.

Arturo caught the look. 'Is something troubling you, gentlemen? Can we be of assistance?'

Somehow a hotel lobby didn't seem the place to go into things. Far too public, for a start. Besides, it seemed a pity to spoil Arturo's happy mood.

I looked at Dad and gave a tiny shake of my head. Dad obviously agreed. 'There was something we wished to consult you about,' he said. 'Later, perhaps.'

'With the greatest of pleasure,' said Arturo. 'Now we must go. We have arranged for dinner in one of the finest restaurants in Palermo. They will be expecting us . . .'

And indeed they were. The limousine whisked us across town to a restaurant halfway up Monte Pellegrino, just outside the city. As we got out of the car, a distinguished-looking, silver-haired gentleman came down the steps to greet us. He looked like an ambassador at the very least, but turned out to be the manager of the restaurant.

'Professore Baldovino,' he said. 'And Dottore Casale. Such a pleasure to see you again. And this must be the distinguished *professore* from England? And this fine young man is his son? Such an honour for my humble establishment.'

His humble establishment was a palace of snowy-white table linen and glittering chandeliers. He ushered us past squads of bowing waiters to a sort of private alcove with a table for four. Through the window behind the alcove we could see the lights of Palermo below.

Once we were seated the manager said, 'Now, gentlemen, you do not trouble yourselves with the menu. I have selected for you an assortment of our finest food and wines. We begin with some simple *antipasti* . . .'

Eventually the enormous meal came to an end and little cups of strong black espresso coffee were brought.

I sat there in a sort of well-fed glow, thinking that all we needed now was a footman with a tray of Ferrero Rocher. But under the surface, the worry about the events of the afternoon was still there. Since hearing Arturo's news, I'd been thinking things over – and had been brooding over the problem all through the meal. By now I'd come up with a theory that made me more worried than ever.

I looked enquiringly at Dad, wondering if now was the time to speak.

Arturo, who was a lot sharper than he appeared, caught the look. 'You mentioned some problem,' he said gently. 'If there is any way in which we can be of assistance . . .'

Dad cleared his throat. 'My son had a some-what disturbing experience this afternoon. Perhaps it's better if he tells you about it himself. Matthew?'

Once again I went through my story. It sounded even stranger the second time. Arturo and Fabio listened attentively until I'd finished.

Arturo maintained a thoughtful silence. Fabio, however, did exactly what Dad hadn't done – he started to pour scorn on my story.

'You are sure that it was really a rocket-launcher you saw – not just some piece of building equipment? A drainpipe perhaps, or a drill?'

'It was definitely a weapon of some kind. If it was innocent building equipment why did the men chase after me?'

Fabio shrugged. 'You said they had a couple of accidents? First the van hit the gatepost, then they dropped the whatever-it-was from their van?'

'That's right.'

'And then they looked up and saw you watching them?'

'I suppose so.'

'Were you laughing?'

I thought for a moment. 'I suppose I may have looked a bit amused. There'd been a lot of banging and yelling and carrying on.'

'Exactly!' said Fabio triumphantly. 'Sicilian men are very proud. These two have a couple of humiliating accidents, they make fools of them-selves – and they look up to see some foreign tourist laughing at them! Naturally they chased you off!'

'They didn't just chase me off, they searched the street for me afterwards. And they tried to pull me out of a moving taxi. That's a lot of reaction just for hurt pride.'

'We Sicilians are a fiery, passionate race,' said

Fabio. 'What might seem overreaction to you could be normal for us!'

I shook my head. 'I'm sorry, I just don't buy it. Besides, I know what I saw – and I saw some kind of weapon. A rocket-launcher or an anti-tank gun.'

Dad came to my aid. 'I don't know if you are aware that I am currently the director of a paranormal research department? Matthew has been acting as my assistant. He is a highly trained observer and I've always found him a completely reliable witness.'

First I've heard of it! I thought. Feather-headed wild goose-chaser was his normal line. But I was grateful for the support all the same.

Dad turned to Arturo, who had been silent all this time. 'What do you think, Professor Baldovino?'

'I believe the boy,' said Arturo. 'Sadly, weapons of every kind are not uncommon in Palermo. But as to the significance of the information . . .'

'What do you mean?' asked Dad.

'All we could tell the police is that some unknown men, possibly Mafiosi, are in possession of a dangerous military weapon. I imagine the police may well be aware of that already. But what these men propose to do with this weapon, and when . . .' He spread his hands. 'Of that we know nothing!'

'Exactly,' said Fabio. 'Maybe some over-ambitious Mafioso plans to shell the headquarters of a rival. Let the swine blow each other up, I say! What do we care?'

'They may be planning to blow up somebody considerably more important,' I said. 'Somebody we do care about.'

'I suppose it's a possibility,' said Dad. 'As Professore Baldovino says, we have no idea of their real plans.'

'Perhaps we do,' I said.

Dad looked at me in surprise. 'Matthew?'

I turned to Arturo. 'I've been thinking, ever since you told us the news – about Senator Lupo coming to the university. Suppose that news and what happened to me are connected?'

Arturo looked astonished. 'How could they be?'

I produced a tourist map of Palermo from my blazer pocket and spread it out on the table. Everyone craned their head to look. I took out a pencil. 'Here's the university, right?' I marked the spot with a little cross. I looked at Arturo. 'I take it this senator has an office somewhere?'

He nodded. 'The headquarters of the commission are in the town centre.'

I handed him the pencil. 'Could you mark it, please? Approximately will do.'

Arturo squinted at the map and made another little cross.

'And where does he live?' I asked.

'He has a detached villa in the countryside outside Palermo. They say it is like a fortress.'

'Will you mark that too, please?'

Arturo made another cross, this time on the edge of the city.

I took back the pencil, and peered at the map. 'As near as I can work out, I walked to about *here* this afternoon.' I pointed with the pencil.

Arturo looked at the map. 'Via Pietro. There is certainly a street market. I sometimes buy my vegetables there.'

'Right,' I said. I made another cross.

'I trust there is some point to this,' said Dad acidly.

'Bear with me,' I said. 'I'm a highly trained observer, remember?'

Using a butter-knife as a ruler, I drew a line from the senator's office to the university. Then I drew a second line from his villa to the university.

The lines met at the university, forming a V-shape. At the very bottom of the V, close to the university itself, was the cross I'd marked myself. The warehouse where I'd seen the rocket-launcher.

Dad got the idea at once, and gave a sharp intake of breath.

The others still looked baffled, so I spelled it out. 'Whether the senator comes from his villa or his office, his route will take him close to the yard where I saw the weapon. And the yard is in front of a very tall warehouse. I imagine you can see all the surrounding streets from the top.' I paused. 'So – a man up on the roof with binoculars and a rocket-launcher, looking for a particular official car . . .'

They got it then all right. Their reactions were very different.

'This is nonsense!' spluttered Fabio. 'Pure speculation.'

Arturo shook his head. 'No, no, the boy is right. Somehow I am sure of it. They are planning to assassinate the senator – on the day he visits our university!

Chapter Four

THE SENATOR

There was a lot of arguing after that – and plenty of objections. Most of them came from Fabio, who insisted it was just a case of an exaggerated imagination – mine.

'If we go to the authorities with this ridiculous story the senator will cancel his visit. The closing ceremony will be ruined, the university will be shamed. We shall fail to honour our distinguished guest here as he deserves.'

'Don't worry about me,' said Dad. 'Anyway, I can't get an honorary degree from a dead senator.'

But even Dad had doubts. 'There's no guarantee the senator will take the direct route, Matthew,' he said.

'You're forgetting one of the most basic laws of mathematics,' I said.

'Indeed? Which one?'

'The one about a straight line being the shortest

distance between two points,' I said. 'I doubt if the senator will go zigzagging all over Palermo when he knows the Mafia are after him. Besides, any route he takes has got to end up at the university – and that warehouse commands all possible approaches.'

'We must warn the authorities at once,' said Arturo. 'It is the only thing we can do.'

'We were hoping you would help us to do it discreetly,' I said. 'Introduce us to the right person to tell.'

Suddenly Fabio jumped up. 'Leave it to me,' he said. 'I have a cousin in the Ministry of Justice. He will know what to do. I will call him at once!' He jumped up and headed for the door.

The ambassador-like manager headed Fabio off halfway, obviously asking if he could help. He pointed back to the table but Fabio shook his head and marched out of the door.

'Well, there's a sudden conversion,' I said.

'Fabio is a good fellow,' said Arturo loyally. 'Just a little impulsive, that's all. He will help us if he can.'

'He seems very young for his position,' I said. 'Is he a particularly distinguished scholar?'

It was hard to imagine the elegant, Armani-suited Fabio bashing the books.

Arturo smiled and spread his hands. 'Well . . . Let us say rather that he is well-connected. I'm afraid that is how things are done here.'

'It's how things are done in a lot of places,' said Dad.'I remember once in America . . .'

He and Arturo exchanged academic gossip until Fabio came hurrying back. 'My cousin has left his office, and cannot be reached tonight. He will be there first thing in the morning. I will call him then.'

Dad and I might have left it at that, but Arturo wasn't having any. The tubby little professor was a lot more determined than he looked. 'No!' he snapped. 'The delay is not acceptable. I will inform the senator directly. I shall call him at his villa.'

'Really?' said Fabio. 'Do you have the number? I imagine it is restricted.'

'As it happens I do,' said Arturo triumphantly. 'The senator called me this evening to discuss his visit. As it happened, I was temporarily unavailable and he left a number for me to call back.'

Arturo looked round and waved, and the manager came hurrying anxiously over. 'Is there some problem, *signori*?'

'Simply a tiresome matter of business,' said Arturo. 'My compliments on a truly superb meal.'

We all gave murmurs of agreement.

'The *professore* is very kind,' said the manager. 'Now, how may I serve you?'

'If I could have a telephone?'

The manager raised a hand and made one of those complicated Italian gestures. A waiter came hurrying over with a white telephone, plugged it in a nearby wall-socket and placed it on the table before Arturo. The manager and the waiter bowed and withdrew.

Arturo took out a notebook, opened it, and dialled a number. He listened for a moment and then began to speak in rapid Italian.

I listened, thinking again how much you could take in without knowing the language. Arturo spoke too quickly for me to follow a single word. Yet somehow it was perfectly clear that he was apologising for disturbing the person on the other end of the line, and asking some kind of favour.

Finally he nodded in satisfaction and said, '*Grazie, senatore, molto grazie.*' He put down the telephone and looked triumphantly around the table. 'We are invited to visit the senator at his villa for an after-dinner drink.'

'Well done,' said Dad, and I nodded agreement.

Fabio, however, felt differently. 'I must beg you to excuse me,' he said stiffly. 'I cannot agree with the wisdom of your proposed course of action. Besides, I have a good deal of work to do before tomorrow. Please feel free to take the car. I will ask the manager to call me a taxi.'

'As you wish, my dear Fabio,' said Arturo cheerfully. I had the distinct feeling he was glad to be rid of him. So was I. At least we'd be able to show the senator a united front.

Arturo settled the bill and the three of us made our way out of the restaurant, escorted by the silver-haired manager in a flurry of thanks and compliments.

I glanced quickly back just as we left the room. The telephone was still on the table and Fabio was talking into it urgently. Maybe he was ordering his taxi . . .

The limousine whisked us down the mountain, through Palermo and up to the gates of a lonely villa on a country road.

The villa was invisible, completely surrounded by a high wall. There was barbed-wire running along the top of the wall.

The limousine stopped before a heavy iron door. Arturo got out and spoke into an intercom set beside the gate. After a brief exchange the gate swung open and we drove through to a cobbled yard in front of the house.

Half a dozen tough-looking young men in leather jackets appeared from nowhere and surrounded the car. Two of them carried rifles and the other four kept their hands near the bulges under their left shoulders.

Slowly we got out of the car.

'Please be patient,' said Arturo. 'They are a little nervous these days.'

They're nervous! I thought.

Taking care to move slowly, Arturo produced identification papers. One of the young men examined them, gave them back, and then patted him down for weapons.

Two other young men approached me and Dad and did the same for us. Dad didn't like it much, but he put up with it patiently.

One of the young men beckoned us to follow

him and we went inside the house. We walked along a gloomy corridor and he showed us into a comfortable, shabby sitting-room filled with heavy, old-fashioned furniture.

There were four people in the room: a big man, a small, fair woman and two children, a boy of about ten and a girl of about six. They were sitting round a big oak table playing some kind of card game. It seemed to be some Sicilian equivalent of Snap. The kids were slamming down their cards and yelling with excitement.

The tall man shushed them and came over to greet us. Arturo made introductions in rapid Italian.

I suppose I'd been expecting someone smooth and sophisticated like the restaurant manager. But Senator Lupo was a big, shaggy-looking man with the heavy, rawboned build of a peasant. He had a craggy face with a strong jaw, a heavy moustache and bushy eyebrows. I suddenly remembered that *lupo* was Italian for wolf.

I'd been prepared for a lot of tedious translation but, like Arturo and Fabio, the senator spoke excellent English. 'This is my wife Maria,' he said. 'My daughter Paola and my son Giorgio.'

The woman smiled shyly and the kids stared curiously at us.

'My son, Matthew,' said Dad.

Lupo and I shook hands. He had a grip like a steel clamp. Then he shook hands with Dad and said how honoured he was to meet him. 'The honour is all mine, senator,' said Dad. He can be charming when he likes, and I could see he had taken to Lupo.

Lupo turned to Arturo. 'And to what do I owe the pleasure of this unexpected visit, *professore*?'

Arturo glanced quickly at the senator's wife and two children. 'A small problem about the arrangements for your visit, senator. I'm sorry to disturb your evening, but I thought it best to clear up the matter in person.'

Lupo took his cue. 'Perhaps we'd better talk in my study.' He said something apologetic in Italian to his wife and children and led us out of the room.

We followed him along the corridor – where a watchful bodyguard stood waiting – and into a room with a desk and a safe and more old-fashioned furniture.

He settled us into chairs and went to a drinks cabinet. 'I have English whisky,' he said proudly.

'A grateful state supplies me with every luxury.'

He served Dad, Arturo and himself with large whiskies and looked doubtfully at me.

'I don't suppose there's any chance of a Coke?' I asked.

Dad shuddered, but Lupo grinned. 'My bodyguards drink it all the time. They have great admiration for all things American.'

He yelled something in Italian and a few minutes later a bodyguard appeared with an ice-cold can of Coke.

'I must apologise for all the melodrama surrounding your visit,' said Lupo when the bodyguard had gone. 'Things in Palermo have suddenly become rather volatile.'

'I thought things had quietened down,' said Arturo.

'They did for a while,' said Lupo. 'Thanks to the *penitenti* we've been hitting the Mafia hard.'

'Penitents?' asked Dad.

'It is our elaborate Italian name for what do you say – squealers,' said Lupo. 'Captured Mafiosi who have broken *omerta*, the sacred code of silence, and informed on their fellows, in return for a lighter sentence.'

'At first there were only one or two,' said Arturo. 'Recently there has been a positive flood of them.'

'The Mafia have been under too much pressure to attack police and public officials,' Lupo continued. 'But now they've suddenly started killing each other. There seems to be a new Mafia war beginning. There's a rumour that a new young challenger, called Primo, is trying to take over from Don Corvino and the rest of the older Mafiosi.'

'As a matter of fact,' I said, 'we've got a rather melodramatic reason for coming to see you.'

Lupo looked at me in surprise.

'Professor Stirling's son had a rather disturbing experience this afternoon,' said Arturo. 'We thought it our duty to inform you of it. Matthew?'

I drew a deep breath and told my story for the third time that day. The walk, the accident with the van, the rocket-launcher falling from the back, the pursuit by the two men and my escape in the taxi.

Lupo sat listening expressionlessly. When I'd finished he asked quietly, 'Is that all?'

'It's all the hard facts,' I said. 'I know I saw a rocket-launcher and not a drainpipe or a drill.'

'Oh, I believe you,' said Lupo calmly. 'We

received a report from Interpol that such a device had been stolen from an American base. What makes you so sure it was taken for my benefit?'

'I've got a theory if you'd care to listen.'

I produced my map and showed the crosses, pointing out how the warehouse covered the last part of every possible route to the university. 'If they knew the time you were due to arrive,' I said. 'And if they know your car . . .'

Lupo nodded appreciatively. 'It's an excellent plan, it might work very well. You would make a good Mafioso, young man.'

I shuddered. 'I hope not!'

'It was meant as a compliment, Matthew,' he said solemnly. 'To defeat them one must learn how to think like them.'

'Do you really think they would go to such lengths?' asked Dad.

'Oh yes,' said Lupo. 'Do you know how they killed one of my most illustrious predecessors? They filled an entire viaduct with several tons of explosive. Then they blew up his car as it passed over the viaduct on the way to the airport. They killed the man they were after, his wife and child and three of his bodyguards.'

I thought of Lupo's wife and two kids in the nearby room, and wondered what it was like to live, every day, in the shadow of death.

'It is possible that you and your son are in some danger,' Lupo went on. 'Not very likely, to be honest, but possible. If you wish to cut short your visit and return to London, I can provide an escort to get you safely to the airport.'

'Avoiding any exploding viaducts on the way?' I said.

Lupo smiled grimly. 'I don't think they would go to so much trouble for you. Your involvement is only marginal.' He turned to Dad. 'Well, professor? If you wish I can have your luggage collected from your hotel and put you on a plane to London tonight.'

It sounded like a good offer to me and I half-hoped Dad would accept – but I knew he wouldn't.

'No,' he said. 'You said yourself the danger is only slight. And if I let them chase me away then they've won. But perhaps you ought to leave, Matthew. You have no commitment to the university – and you're the one with the danger-ous knowledge.'

'No!' I heard myself saying. 'If you stay, I stay.'

'Well, there you are,' said Dad. 'It seems that we can't accept your generous offer. But your own position is very different, senator. You are in constant danger, and there's no point in taking unnecessary risks. I think you should cancel your visit to the university.'

'And what about you, professor?'

'I'll be happy to leave straight after my third and final lecture. You can send me my honorary degree by registered post!'

Lupo shook his head. 'What was it you said a moment ago? If I let them chase me away they've won! Besides, we can at least put an end to this particular plan.' He bellowed something in Italian and the hovering bodyguard reappeared. Lupo shot out a stream of orders, annexing my tourist map and handing it over.

The bodyguard said, '*Immediatamente, senatore!*' and vanished.

'He will liaise with the *carabinieri* and raid the warehouse,' said Lupo.

I shook my head. 'They won't find anything. Not now the Mafiosi know they were seen.'

Lupo frowned. 'But if we drive them and their weapon away from the warehouse . . .'

'The whole point about the rocket-launcher is that it's portable,' I said. 'Two men can carry it easily. If they take it away they can bring it back!'

'We can seal off the warehouse.'

'There may still be other vantage points.'

'We will search them and then seal them off as well!'

'That's more like it,' I said. 'And search all possible hiding-places as well. The best thing would be to capture that rocket-launcher.'

'I'll give orders at once,' said Lupo. 'Anything else?'

'Yes. I think you ought to send an empty official car to the ceremony and smuggle yourself into the university some other way . . .'

I suddenly realised that Dad and Arturo were watching this conversation like spectators at a tennis match, turning their heads from one side to the other.

Dad was getting fed up with it. 'If you've quite finished arranging everything to your satisfaction, Matthew,' he said irritably. He hates not being the centre of attention.

'Only trying to be helpful,' I said.

Lupo clapped me on the shoulder, nearly

knocking me off my chair. 'And so you are. I shall consider all you have said. We can discuss it tomorrow. If you don't want to be a Mafioso, maybe you'd care for a job with the Anti-Mafia Commission?'

I shook my head. 'I like the quiet life.' I looked at Dad. 'Let's get back to investigating some nice spooks. At least they don't shoot at you!'

'Now, if you will forgive me,' said Lupo. 'I promised to finish the card game with my children before their bedtime . . .'

We were silent and thoughtful on the journey back. We had refused Lupo's offer of an escort, and everything seemed peaceful.

The car dropped off Arturo at his flat near the university and then took us to our small but luxurious hotel, which was in a quiet back street. At least it was usually quiet.

As the limousine glided away I suddenly heard the sound of a powerful motorbike. It came roaring towards us at top speed.

I rugby-tackled Dad, bringing us both to the ground. Machinegun bullets rattled above our heads . . .

Chapter Five

KIDNAP

The motorbike roared away and we scrambled to our feet.

'Quick!' I gasped. 'Get inside.'

I shoved frantically at the hotel door. It was locked. My heart sank as I realised why. It's only very big hotels that leave their front doors open at night. Smaller hotels, like this one, lock them. They have an illuminated bell and a night porter, who comes and opens up when you ring the bell.

I jabbed frantically at the night bell but nothing happened. Maybe the night porter was asleep. Maybe he'd heard the gunshots and wasn't coming at all.

I heard the sound of an engine at the far end of the street, somewhere to our left. It was getting louder.

The big motorbike had turned and was heading towards us again. The killer was coming back for another go. And there was nowhere to hide.

We both stood frozen as the motorbike zoomed nearer. The black-clad, helmeted driver was steering with one hand, clutching a machine-pistol in the other.

Suddenly there was the crack of a single shot. The motorbike veered off-course and crashed into the side of the hotel. The rider was thrown from the saddle and lay sprawled in the gutter.

The bike lay on its side, engine sputtering and wheels spinning.

I looked in the direction of the shot and saw a tall, thin man in a black raincoat at the end of the street. Moonlight gleamed on the big pistol in his hand.

We looked at each other for a moment and then he turned and disappeared round the corner.

The hotel door was open by now and Dad was yelling at the night porter. '*Polizia!* Call the police!'

Drawn by some strange compulsion I went over to look at the sprawled figure of the dead assassin. The fall had knocked the helmet from his head and blood was trickling from a wound in the back of his neck.

He was no older than I was.

* * *

'It is often the way,' said Lupo. 'These days the killers come younger and younger. The Mafia take them off the streets, teach them to shoot, give them guns and send them out to kill. The boys are proud to do it. They think it makes them men.'

We were talking in our hotel suite, some time later. Lupo had picked up the police report of the attempted shooting, and turned up with a squad of his bodyguards to make sure we were all right.

'Still, I'm glad you ignored us and sent a body-guard after all,' I said.

Lupo stared at me. 'But I didn't. To be honest, I didn't think you were in any real danger. You had given your information, they had nothing to gain by killing you.'

'Then who shot the boy on the motorbike – and saved our lives?'

Lupo shrugged. 'Some rival Mafioso, perhaps.'

'But why should he help us?'

'I have no idea! I don't even understand why you were attacked in the first place. Forgive me, it isn't even as if your information was vitally important. We already knew the rocket-launcher had been stolen, and was probably in Mafia hands.'

'Sheer nastiness?' I suggested. 'Punishment for spoiling one of their schemes?'

'I suppose so,' said Lupo. 'But it isn't like the Mafia. They usually kill for good business reasons, not petty spite.'

'I'm not interested in *why* we were shot at,' snapped Dad. 'The fact remains that somebody tried to kill us – and may try again. You must see, senator, that this changes everything. I'd like to take advantage of your offer. I want Matthew and myself out of Sicily as soon as possible.'

I didn't argue. It wasn't so much being shot at that had shocked me as the sight of the would-be assassin's face. I didn't want to stay in a place where kids my age were trained to be killers.

'Of course,' said Lupo gravely. 'I have already checked the flights. There is nothing available now until midday tomorrow. I'll see that you are guarded tonight, and have you escorted to the plane in the morning. I am sorry that your visit to Palermo has ended so unhappily.'

We said our goodnights and Lupo went off.

When we were alone I said, 'If you want to stay, Dad, I'm still game.'

He shook his head. 'I don't. I don't intend to

risk my life for an honorary degree – especially when I've got so many proper degrees already!'

I knew it was my life he was thinking about. And since I was worrying about his, there was no more to say. Soon after that, we both went off to bed.

I'd expected to have a restless night but I went off straight away and slept like the proverbial log.

When I woke up next morning, Dad wasn't there.

I was only mildly alarmed at first, assuming he'd gone down to breakfast. Or maybe he'd gone to the university to say his goodbyes.

When there was still no sign of him by the time I'd showered and had a room-service breakfast I started to worry.

And I was puzzled by the fact that there was no guard outside our door.

With the help of the English-speaking hotel telephone operator I managed to place a call to Senator Lupo.

'I had a message from your father late last night,' he said. 'He told me he'd changed his mind, decided he'd overreacted, and that the danger was probably over. He asked me to withdraw my guards and cancel today's flight. He said he'd see me tomorrow at the ceremony.'

'How did he sound?'

'A little strained, perhaps, but after the events of last night that's only natural.'

'And you're sure it was Dad?'

'Absolutely. I recognised his voice. He complimented me on my whisky, and made some joke about your addiction to Coke. It was definitely him, Matthew. Is anything wrong?'

'Probably not. It's just that I overslept a bit and he doesn't seem to be around.'

'He said he was going to the university,' said Lupo. 'Call me if he doesn't turn up soon.'

I promised I would and put down the phone.

I sat thinking for a moment. Dad cheerfully shrugging off a Mafia machinegunning and deciding to stay on? Then wandering off to the university without saying goodbye or even leaving a note?

No way.

I put on jeans, trainers, a sweatshirt and a denim jacket, and felt much more like myself.

I picked up the telephone and got the operator to call me a taxi.

* * *

When I tracked down Professore Arturo Baldovino in his shabby and untidy office at the university, he sounded almost as surprised as Lupo.

'But your father telephoned me this morning, Matthew. He told me of the shocking events of last night, and said that although he had changed his mind about leaving, he didn't feel up to delivering today's lecture. He asked me to cancel it, with apologies, and announce that he would condense his second and third lectures into one, which he would deliver tomorrow.'

Arturo spread his hands. 'So – that is what I have done! Everyone has been most understanding.'

I knew the answer to my next question, but I had to ask. 'And you're sure it was him?'

'Of course. He told me how much he had enjoyed meeting Senator Lupo, and said he was looking forward to the award ceremony. Is anything wrong, Matthew?'

I assured him everything was fine, and asked for directions to Fabio's office.

'I just want to say hello,' I said.

I found Dottore Fabio Casale in a smaller but more luxuriously furnished office just along the corridor from Arturo. He looked up from a big, ornate desk as I strode into his office, slamming the door behind me.

'Oh, it's you, Matthew. Don't they teach you to knock in England? I can't talk to you now, I'm busy.'

'Too bad,' I said. 'You'll talk to me now and like it.'

He jumped to his feet. 'This is outrageous. Get out of my office!'

As I mentioned before, I'm big and strong for my age. I was a lot bigger and stronger than Fabio, and I was good and mad. I grabbed him by his elegantly-tailored shoulders and slammed him back in his chair, so hard that it bounced back against the wall.

'Now, Fabio,' I said. 'Where's my father?'

He looked up at me, wild-eyed. 'How should I know?'

'Because I'm pretty sure he's been kidnapped,' I said. 'And you're tied in with the Mafia.'

'That is an absurd accusation!'

'Is it?' I said grimly. 'Last night in the restaurant you only pretended to phone your cousin in the ministry. You were stalling, playing for time. That's why you insisted on going off to phone, instead of having one brought to the table.'

'I was not aware that it was possible . . .'

'Rubbish. The manager tried to tell you. Arturo knew, and you're both regulars at that restaurant. When Arturo insisted on calling the senator, you stayed behind to call your Mafia friends. You told them where we were going and why. You're responsible for the attempt to kill us.'

I could feel myself getting angry again and I loomed over him threateningly. 'Arturo said you had influence,' I went on. 'In Palermo, influence means Mafia.'

Fabio shrank back. 'Look, Matthew, I can explain everything. Let me show you . . .'

He slid his chair back to the desk and opened a top drawer. I grabbed a heavy ebony ruler from his desk and slammed him across the knuckles with it. He gave a yelp of pain and snatched back his hand. I reached into the open drawer and took out a small black automatic. It was a Beretta. The kind M made James Bond give up in *Dr No*.

'A ladies' gun,' I said. 'I'm surprised at you, Fabio.' I aimed it between his eyes. 'You must have some pretty tough classes here.'

I didn't even know if the safety-catch was on or

off. Fabio didn't know either. 'I can't tell you anything,' he babbled. 'Primo will kill me.'

'I'll kill you if you don't talk,' I said. 'Who's Primo?'

'His name is DeMitri, Arrigo DeMitri. He calls himself Primo now.'

I remembered Lupo talking about an up-and-coming young Mafioso.

I waved the gun. 'Has he kidnapped my father?'

'I don't know,' he sobbed. 'I swear I don't know.'

'Then find out,' I said. 'Find out by tonight, or I'll turn you in to Lupo. Understand?'

'All right,' said Fabio miserably. He took out his wallet and handed me an engraved card. 'This is my address, come round this evening. If I find out anything I'll tell you then.'

I stuck his card and his gun in my pocket and went out of the office. I walked out of the university with my mind in a whirl, wondering what to do next.

I suppose I should have got someone at the university to call me a taxi, but I wanted time to think.

I started walking in what I hoped was the direction of the hotel, and soon realised I was lost.

I felt for my tourist map of Palermo, and remembered that Lupo had taken it.

I looked round for a taxi, but there was nothing in sight.

Then suddenly my problem was solved for me. A black limousine pulled up beside me and the driver reached back and opened the rear passenger door.

'Get in.'

I looked hard at him. Last time I'd seen him he'd been standing in the street by my hotel with an outsized pistol in his hand. He was the mysterious gunman who had saved both our lives.

'Please, get in,' he said softly. His English was strongly accented, but very fluent. 'I don't mean you any harm. I could have killed you last night. I could have done nothing and *watched* you get killed last night. You owe me.'

There was no arguing with that. I got into the car. I closed the door and it drew away.

'Where are we going?' I asked.

'It's a surprise,' he said.

It was certainly that.

The car took me through Palermo, up the lower slopes of Monte Pellegrino and finally through the gates of a superb white villa overlooking the bay.

The gunman parked the car on the gravel drive, watched by a couple of shotgun-carrying guards. One of them routinely patted me down, discovering and removing Fabio's Beretta. Then he led me up a flight of marble steps at the side of the house and along a terrace crowded with colourful and exotic flowers.

There was an alcove at the end of the terrace with a superb view of the bay. In it was a table with a big central umbrella. Two men sat at the table, sipping wine. There was a bottle in an ice bucket on the table.

One of the men was old and fat with a face like a Roman emperor and a great bald head fringed with white hair. He wore black trousers and a white shirt.

The other was my father.

He looked up as I came along the terrace.

'Ah, there you are at last! Don Corvino, this is my son Matthew. Matthew, allow me to introduce Don Corvino. He is by way of being the Godfather of the local Mafia, and he wishes to employ our services . . .'

* * *

Chapter Six

THE ASSIGNMENT

I sat down at the table.

Dad reached into the ice bucket and took out a can of Coke. They'd been expecting me all right.

I opened the can of Coke and sipped it, looking hard at Dad. I sensed that underneath his apparent calm he was seething with rage. It was scarcely surprising. First he'd been shot at, and now kidnapped. But the anger was all under tight control.

I remembered the old saying, *Don't get mad, get even.* Dad was playing it cool – and if he could, then so could I.

I looked at the other man. He wasn't much to look at – just a big, white-haired old man enjoying a glass of wine in his garden. But he was somebody all the same. You could feel the force of his personality.

'I am happy to welcome you to my house,' he said.

He spoke in a soft, wheezing voice and his English, like that of his gunman, was heavily accented but fluent. I'd read somewhere that English was the language of international business. Perhaps it was also the language of international crime.

Dad spoke again, still with that same unnatural calm. 'Don Corvino assures me that he had nothing to do with the plan to assassinate Senator Lupo. Nor indeed with the attempt to kill us. Both were the work of one of his business rivals.'

'Someone called Primo,' I said.

Don Corvino's eyes widened. 'You are well informed.'

Scared as I was, I gave a modest shrug and tried to look as if the secrets of the Mafia were an open book to me.

'Don Corvino wishes our help in dealing with this man,' said Dad. 'That is why he brought me here.'

'And those phonecalls to Senator Lupo and Arturo . . . ?' I asked.

'Don Corvino persuaded me to make the calls,' said Dad through gritted teeth. 'He told me it would be better for your health if I did as he asked.'

I nodded, understanding why Dad was so angry. If there was one thing he hated it was giving way to threats. But with me alone and unprotected he'd had no choice.

Don Corvino could control either of us, simply by threatening the other.

'A regrettable necessity,' wheezed Don Corvino. 'Please accept my apologies. Now, permit me to explain why I need your help.' He took another sip of wine. 'The affairs of Cosa Nostra – we prefer the term to Mafia – are at a critical stage. We have suffered defeats by the law, and there have been too many internal struggles. It is a time for retrenchment, to keep our heads down while we rebuild our strength. Such rash actions as the assassination of government officials will only bring more trouble on our heads.'

'But not everybody sees it that way?' I suggested.

'Men of respect, such as myself, are all agreed,' rumbled Don Corvino. 'But there is a younger element, led by this man Primo. They kill wantonly, without purpose. Government officials, police, even fellow Mafiosi, it makes no difference to them.' He gave an indignant glare. 'They even tried to assassinate *me*!'

'Shocking,' I said. 'But I still don't understand why you want our help. We're not hitmen, we investigate the paranormal.'

'That is precisely why I need you. I was already aware through my own sources of your successes in the paranormal field. It is a subject in which I have always taken great interest. As soon as I heard you were coming to Palermo, I felt that you were the answer to all my problems.'

'I still don't understand why,' I said. 'What possible connection is there between the Mafia – sorry, Cosa Nostra – and the paranormal?'

'It is very simple,' said Don Corvino. 'This Primo has no background in Cosa Nostra, no family connections. He came from nowhere and rose incredibly rapidly. He exercises great power over his followers. They are all young men, like himself, many are even younger, no more than boys.'

I nodded, thinking of the dead gunman outside the hotel.

'He sends them on suicide missions and they go without question,' Don Corvino went on. 'The boy who tried to kill me walked on into the gunfire of my guards as if his life meant nothing to him. It is rumoured that Primo can strike a man dead simply by pointing his finger. He seems immune to any attack. The men I have have sent to kill him have all died horrible deaths. How does he achieve all this?'

I shrugged again. 'Search me.'

'I believe he has supernatural powers,' said Don Corvino earnestly. 'That is why I need your help.'

Even Dad was amazed. 'My dear sir, are you serious?'

'Perfectly. Sicily is an island with a very long history. There are ancient temples here going back to the time of the Greeks and the Romans, places of great power. There are old women, witches, in the hills with the power of the evil eye. This Primo is *maledetto*, accursed. He has sold his soul to the devil. He has defences I cannot pass, powers I cannot match. You must destroy him for me. Or at least, discover his weaknesses so that I can destroy him.'

'All right,' I said. 'We'll do our best to help you – you don't leave us much choice. But you'll have to let us go. We can do nothing if we're kept prisoners here.'

'I will have to let one of you go,' corrected Don Corvino blandly. 'One must remain here as my guest, to ensure the loyalty of the other.' He turned to Dad. 'You, sir, will stay. This is a young man's business and we old fellows must remain on the sidelines.'

Dad argued furiously, but Don Corvino wouldn't listen.

'Suppose when I leave here I go straight to Senator Lupo?' I asked.

'Suppose you do? In due course he will arrive here with a squad of *carabinieri* and search my villa. But he will not find your father – and you will never see him again.'

There was a chilling conviction in his words.

I nodded, accepting the inevitable. 'All right. I'll see what I can do.'

'Excellent,' said Don Corvino. He clapped his hands and became the perfect host. 'And now, let me offer you some lunch . . .'

An hour later I was back in the black limousine, chauffeured by Don Corvino's hatchet-faced gunman. He stopped outside our hotel and I got out.

The gunman looked impassively at me for a

moment. 'Good luck. You're going to need it.'

The limousine swept away and I went into the hotel.

I called Professore Arturo Baldovino at the university and persuaded him to come and see me as soon as he was free. Then I sat on the bed, thinking about my impossible assignment. How could I possibly find this Primo? And what could I do if I did?

When Arturo arrived I swore him to secrecy and told him the whole story. He was horrified. 'Your father kidnapped? We must tell the police! We must go to Senator Lupo!'

I shook my head. 'It wouldn't do any good.'

A sudden thought struck me. Fabio hadn't told me much – but he'd told me Primo's real name.

'Do you know anything about someone called DeMitri?' I asked. 'Arrigo DeMitri?'

'Oh yes,' said Arturo. 'He was a student here for quite some time. He came from one of Sicily's most distinguished families. They lost all their money after the war. Arrigo was always very bitter about it.'

'Do you know what happened to him?'

'He was expelled for blasphemy, I think,' said Arturo. 'Something to do with forbidden dabbling in the occult.'

'Do you know the sort of thing he was looking into?' I asked.

Arturo shook his head. 'We could soon find out, though. If we go to the university library we can check what books he took out on their computer. You could look at some of the same books.'

Arturo drove me to the library in his surprisingly snazzy red sports car and I spent the next few hours wading through a variety of sinister occult texts.

It seemed that Arrigo, now Primo, had been particularly interested in the worship of Diana, goddess of the moon.

The book he'd taken out most was about the cult of Diana that was still active in Sicily. It was centred on an ancient temple at a place called Segesta. According to the book, the priestesses of the cult survived as wise women, or witches, feared and revered by the local countryfolk.

By the time I'd finished checking Arrigo's reading-list, it was time for my appointment with Fabio. I knew now that he had nothing to do with Dad's kidnapping. But perhaps I could make him tell me more about Primo.

I persuaded Arturo to drive me there.

Fabio lived in a trendy new block in the centre of Palermo. We went up to his apartment, and found the door slightly ajar. We went inside and saw Fabio sprawled across his designer sofa. There was a small round hole in the centre of his forehead and a bundle of lire notes stuffed into his mouth.

'It's a traditional Mafia message,' said Arturo. 'It means that he talked too much.'

I was silent for a moment, remembering that poor old Fabio had done his talking to me.

'Poor Fabio,' said Arturo. 'To be honest, I never liked him much – but to end like this! We must call the police.'

'No time,' I said. 'I have to go to the temple at Segesta.'

'Tonight?'

'Yes, tonight.'

'Why?'

'The place is important to Primo in some way,' I said. 'I know it's a long shot, but with Fabio dead it's the only clue I have.'

'But it's the night of the full moon!'

'So much the better,' I said. 'All the more reason to go!'

Arturo wasn't happy but I reminded him that he was a modern academic, far too civilised to fear ancient goddesses and pagan spells, and he agreed to drive me there in the end.

Trapani is a small town on the coast not far from Palermo.

About thirty kilometres west of Trapani is the ancient temple of Segesta.

Ancient as it is, the temple with its circle of stone pillars looks surprisingly intact.

We arrived there late that evening and drove into the carpark at the bottom of the hill. It was already beginning to get dark.

'I'll wait for you here,' said Arturo. 'Until you come back – if you do. I'm sorry but I daren't go any further. Not after dark, on the night of the full moon.'

I patted his shoulder. 'Don't worry, you've already done more than I had any right to ask. If I don't come back, go to Senator Lupo and tell him everything.'

I got out of the car to set off up the hill. There was a little café on the far side of the carpark. Although it was late, the café was still open.

On a sudden impulse I went inside. I bought an espresso from the sulky girl behind the counter, and looked around.

There was only one other customer in the café – a thin, black-haired girl in a filmy, flowing white dress. She had huge dark eyes, and was attractive in a weird, off-beat kind of way.

I can't explain it, but I had the oddest feeling that she was waiting for me, that we were destined to meet.

I carried my coffee over to her table. 'May I sit with you?'

I spoke in English without thinking and she replied in the same language. 'If you are not afraid.'

'Why should I be afraid?'

'Because I am a witch,' she said seriously. 'A witch and the granddaughter of a witch.'

I nodded. 'Of course you are.'

It was the night of the full moon and I was visiting an ancient temple. Meeting a witch seemed perfectly natural.

The girl seemed annoyed that I wasn't more impressed. She pointed to the girl at the counter. 'You do not believe me? Look at that girl.'

'What about her?'

'It grows dark, and she is very frightened. She would like to close the café and go home.'

'Then why doesn't she?'

'She doesn't dare,' said the girl grandly. 'Not until *I* am ready to leave!'

I sipped my espresso. 'Not much of an achievement for a full-blown witch, is it, frightening a little café waitress? Is that the best you can do?'

Her eyes flashed with rage. 'I can do more than you dare imagine! Beware my anger.'

I laughed. 'What will you do? Turn me into a toad? It might be quite peaceful being a toad. Nothing to do but sit in the sun and stick out your tongue and catch flies.'

She scowled, but somehow the scowl turned into a smile against her will. 'You do not fear me,' she said, half amused and half angry. 'Everyone fears us! Why are you not afraid?'

There was something strange, even uncanny about her, but for some reason I wasn't really frightened. 'It's hard to be afraid of a pretty girl no older than I am myself. And I've been frightened so much these last few days that my supply of scared has run out.'

'Tell me,' she said commandingly, and for some reason I did. Everything that had happened since we came to Palermo.

When I had finished she said, 'And why do you come here?'

'To visit the temple.'

'Tonight – on the night of the full moon? And you're still not afraid?'

'I suppose so,' I said. 'But I have to go all the same.'

'Why?' she challenged.

'To make an ending,' I heard myself saying. 'It began here, and here is where it must end.'

Don't ask me what I meant.

'And what if the end is your own?'

I shrugged. 'Then that is how it must be.'

She stood up in one sudden, lithe movement. 'Do you really wish to come with me to the temple? I warn you, my grandmother will be there.'

'I'm sure she's a charming old lady,' I said. 'I'd be happy to meet your family.'

'My grandmother is the most powerful witch in

all Sicily! Are you mad?'

'I'm English,' I said. 'Some people think it comes to much the same thing!'

I followed her from the café.

As we passed by the girl at the till she crossed herself. Then she made another gesture, a quick movement of the hand with crossed fingers. I knew what it meant.

It was a sign to avert evil, far older than Christianity.

We came out of the café and began to climb the hill. In her white, robe-like dress the girl seemed to float over the rough ground.

It was almost dark now, and a full moon was rising behind the temple . . .

Chapter Seven

THE POWER

The full moon had risen by the time we reached the circle of stone columns.

An old woman stood waiting.

She was very tall and very thin and she wore long black robes. Grey hair streamed behind her in the wind.

She said something in rapid Italian, her voice a harsh, grating croak. The girl said, 'She says you are not the one. She asks if you have come to seek the Power.'

'Heaven forbid,' I said.

The old woman spoke again, and the girl said, 'She says it is dangerous for you to be here.'

'Tell her I accept the danger.'

The girl spoke and the old woman shrugged her bony shoulders.

We heard footsteps approaching the temple. A man appeared from the other side of the stone circle.

He was young and handsome, dark-eyed and olive-skinned, with thick black curly hair. He wore beautifully cut clothes and expensive-looking leather boots.

He strode arrogantly into the circle and looked around him. He saw me standing between the two women. 'Who are you?' he demanded. 'Why are you here?'

'My name's Matt Stirling,' I said. 'You're Arrigo DeMitri, I presume?'

'My name is Primo. It means first!' he said petulantly. 'You dared to interfere with my plan to kill Lupo, Matt Stirling. For that you will die – now!'

He stretched out a hand towards me – and the girl snapped something in a voice that crackled with anger.

Primo staggered back, as if struck by some invisible force. He recovered and said angrily, 'Your death can wait. Tonight I take on the full Power. No one can save you then.'

Beside me the girl whispered, 'What he says is true. This is the third and final stage. Once he assumes the full Power I can no longer protect you, he will be too strong. Run now, while you can!'

I shook my head. 'No thanks. I'll stay till the end.'

The old woman began to chant and a fiery circle appeared on the stones. Fearlessly Primo stepped inside it.

A wind blew through the temple and a glowing column appeared, bathing the young man in its light.

I had a sudden sensation of tremendous, impersonal power.

In the past I'd sometimes been able to influence events by communicating with alien forces. I suppose I'd hoped to do the same now, but I knew at once that it was hopeless. This was pure psychic power, quite detached from ideas of right or wrong. It would have been like trying to talk to a tornado or an explosion.

The old woman's chanting died down, the wind dropped, the glowing column and the fiery circle faded away.

For a moment Primo stood poised in the centre of the temple. Suddenly he collapsed in a sobbing heap, curling up into a ball.

The old woman walked over to him and looked dispassionately down at the huddled figure. She muttered something to the girl.

'She says his mind has broken beneath the

full Power of the goddess,' said the girl. 'He was arrogant and proud, but inside he was weak.'

The old woman came over to me, stared into my eyes and spoke again.

'She says that you, on the other hand, have the inner strength he lacked. If you care to endure the ritual . . .'

Hurriedly I backed away. 'Tell her thanks but no thanks, it's not my sort of thing at all.'

The girl said something to the old woman in an amused voice. The old woman shrugged and faded away into the darkness.

I looked down at the sobbing Arrigo. He began babbling in a high, childish voice.

'What is he saying?' I asked.

'He says he wants his mother. He's frightened and he wants to go home. He has become as a child.'

'I suppose I'd better take him home, then,' I said wearily. 'Will you give me a hand to get him down the hill? I've got a friend waiting for me – if he hasn't panicked and gone home.'

She said something to Arrigo in a firm voice, and he scrambled to his feet. He held out his hand like a child.

I took his hand and led him down the hill.

Arturo's red sports car was the only car in the carpark, and Arturo was fast asleep behind the wheel. I woke him up and showed him the tearful Arrigo.

'He's had some kind of breakdown,' I said. 'Does he have any family?'

'His mother and sisters are still alive,' said Arturo. 'As a matter of fact, I know them slightly. They live in Palermo.'

'Will you do me a huge favour and take him home?' I said. 'And will you drop me at my hotel on the way? I've an important call to make.'

We loaded Arrigo into the back of the car and he promptly went to sleep.

Arturo got behind the wheel and I turned to say goodbye to the girl.

Before I could speak she suddenly leaned forward and kissed me. Her lips felt burning hot and ice cold at the same time and a sort of fiery tingle ran through me.

'My name is Adriana,' she said. 'You will not forget me.'

'No,' I said feebly. 'I don't think I will.'

She took something from around her neck. It

was a sickle-shaped pendant on a leather thong. The green stone was carved with time-worn symbols. She slipped it over my head.

'Wear this to remind you. It will protect you from evil.'

She faded away into the darkness like a ghost.

I got in the front seat of the car beside Arturo, who had been tactfully looking the other way.

He started the car and we roared away towards Palermo.

Back in the hotel I called the telephone number Don Corvino had given me before I left his villa. He had assured me that it would reach him at any time, night or day.

After a few rings a wheezy voice said, '*Si?*'

'This is Matt Stirling,' I said. 'Your enemy, Primo, no longer exists.'

'You have killed him?' asked the voice eagerly.

'Primo no longer exists,' I repeated. 'You can forget him, he won't give you any more trouble.'

'You tell me this as a man of honour?'

'Upon my honour.'

The wheezy voice replied, 'Your father is on his way back to the hotel.'

He was treating me like a fellow Mafioso. I suppose it was a compliment in a way . . .

The ceremony at the university next morning was a great success.

Dad delivered his condensed two-lectures-in-one to great applause and a standing ovation.

Senator Lupo was there, surrounded by an entourage of watchful young men in dark suits with bulges under their arms. He presented Dad with an ornate scroll – his umpteenth honorary degree.

Afterwards Lupo told me that his men had caught the two Mafiosi with the rocket-launcher, hiding in the basement of an office block near the warehouse.

The Mafiosi had tried to defend themselves with the rocket-launcher. Unfortunately they were carrying it the wrong way round. Apparently Lupo's men thought this was very amusing . . .

Don Corvino was also present amongst the many distinguished guests. He was escorted by his hatchet-faced bodyguard, who gave me a friendly nod.

Corvino and Lupo greeted each other like old friends instead of deadly enemies.

Don Corvino even exchanged a few friendly words with Dad. You'd never have thought they'd been kidnapper and kidnappee. (Dad said afterwards that he'd got quite fond of the old villain. I suspect the fact that Don Corvino kept a cellar full of vintage Chianti had a lot to do with it.)

The ceremonies came to an end at last and we said our goodbyes, including a particularly affectionate farewell from tubby little Arturo.

He said he'd been to see Arrigo and found him sitting on the carpet, playing happily with a box of his old toys.

We'd brought our luggage from the hotel, and soon the limousine arrived to take us to the airport.

I didn't really relax until the plane had taken off. There might still have been some stray Mafioso with a grudge and a machinegun lurking somewhere nearby.

Dad settled himself in his seat and looked hopefully around for the drinks trolley. 'I'm sorry our little trip got you into so much trouble, Matthew,' he said.

I shrugged. 'You're the one who got kidnapped!'

Dad gave me a severe look over the top of his glasses. 'Permit me to point out, however, that if you'd stayed to listen to my first lecture none of this would have happened.'

'I expect something else would have happened, though,' I said.

Suddenly Dad noticed the stone medallion round my neck. 'What on earth is that, Matthew? Some piece of tourist junk? You know I don't approve of jewellery for men! Why don't you take it off?'

'I don't think I'd better,' I said. 'Not till we get home, and maybe not even then. It might not be too safe.'

Dad gave me a baffled glare. 'Why ever not?'

'I'm not sure how to break this to you, Dad,' I said. 'But I think I may be engaged to a witch . . .'